My First Trip

My First Trip to a Farm

Greg Roza

illustrated by
Aurora Aguilera

PowerKiDS press.

New York

Published in 2020 by The Rosen Publishing Group, Inc.
29 East 21st Street, New York, NY 10010

First Edition

Editor: Elizabeth Krajnik
Art Director: Michael Flynn
Book Design: Raúl Rodriguez
Illustrator: Aurora Aguilera

Cataloging-in-Publication Data

Names: Roza, Greg, author.
Title: My first trip to a farm / Greg Roza.
Description: New York : PowerKids Press, [2020] | Series: My first trip |
    Includes index.
Identifiers: LCCN 2018024107| ISBN 9781538344330 (library bound) | ISBN
    9781538345603 (paperback) | ISBN 9781538345610 (6 pack)
Subjects: LCSH: Farms—Juvenile literature. | Farm life—Juvenile literature.
    | Livestock—Juvenile literature.
Classification: LCC S519 .R797 2020 | DDC 630—dc23
LC record available at https://lccn.loc.gov/2018024107

Manufactured in the United States of America

CPSIA Compliance Information: Batch #CSPK19. For further information contact Rosen Publishing, New York, New York at 1-800-237-9932.

Contents

My name is Asher.

This is my best friend, Mateo.

We're going to visit Mateo's uncle.

He's a famer.

I've never been to a farm before.
I wonder what it's like.

We're here!
The farm is huge!

"Hi, Asher. I'm Uncle Lucas."

"Do you want to see the cows?" he asks.

"Yes!" Mateo and I say.

Look at all the cows!

I pet a friendly calf.
She's silly!

Next we see the chickens.

Uncle Lucas let's us feed the chickens.

Uncle Lucas shows us
the sheep.

A worker is removing a sheep's wool.

We visit the horses in the stable.

Uncle Lucas let's us brush
the horses.

Uncle Lucas starts the tractor. It's loud!

We go for a hay ride!

Uncle Lucas makes us lunch.
I like visiting the farm!

Words to Know

calf

stable

tractor

Index